Bli₽.

Rocks and Cotton

Shawn Something

Shawn Something

For my family, friends and a childhood dream.

Shawn Something

<u>Chapter One</u>

A constant breeze filled the land, choreographing the best dance routine any grassy land has seen. It tickled Clemat's hand as he gradually woke up. The breeze tousled his short brown hair, trying to keep up with the steps of the grass around him.

This feels nice, he thought. *The breeze is…. salty?*

Clemat opened his eyes slowly, letting the blurriness fade and the light from the orange clouds fill in. The clouds illuminated the purplish sky behind them which bathed the land in a contrasting purple tinge and orange glow.

"Dang"

Clemat sighed and took out a small moleskin notebook and a pen from his jacket. He flipped to a page with three crudely drawn earths with slash marks over two of them. With his pen, Clemat slashed the third and drew another.

"Here we go again," he said as he rubbed his sore neck.

He stood up, pocketed his notebook, and took a quick look at the grassy plains around him. With a mighty stretch, he started walking and quickly reached a small cliff overlooking a valley.

The orange clouds illuminated the land below. There were huge dandelions that hugged the east of the valley and grew to half the height of the mountains behind them. Below, surrounded by the mountain range, was a small town with houses shaped like coconut husks.

At least I blipped closer to civilization this time. This looks interesting.

He shivered and shook his right foot. Loose hay drifted away from him, finding their place with the land.

"More interesting than a world of hay. That's for sure."
He mumbled while rubbing the back of his neck, the feeling of
a small, non-existent, burning cut faded away as he did.

As he was about to make his way toward the town, a huge
dandelion flew in from the right of his view, quickly moving
above him. It was as tall as a small house and as poofy as any
dandelion would be. On its stem, sat a creature that looked like
a statue made of pebbles.

Clemat looked up in surprise. The pebble person, unaware
of Clemat, was screaming at the top of her rock-like lungs.

"Hey," Clemat said as loudly as he could, in between her
screams "Do you need help? Can you understand me?"

"No no, I'm... Totally in CONTROL!" The small rock
person shouted back at Clemat, unconvincingly.

Just then, the winds caused the dandelion to swirl. The
small rock person held on tight and continued to scream.

"Alright then, have fun." Clemat waved dismissively and
continued walking towards town again. Not even a few steps
in, the dandelion flew above, then behind him. The wind was
not letting up.

BAM!

The base of the dandelion seed knocked him on the back
of his head. Clemat lost balance and tumbled a little down the
slope.

"Woah!" He exclaimed as he was reeling from the impact. He looked up to the dandelion now in front of him with the small rock person at the helm, clearly struggling to hold on.

"Sorry! Guess I'm not really in control!" She said, looking back at Clemat. Her face was etched in the rock, eyes slightly indented and her mouth causing a bump in an otherwise, totally smooth surface. As Clemat locked eyes with her, he could feel that she wasn't filled with fear or regret, but doubt.

"That's it." Clemat picked himself up quickly and ran toward the dandelion, which was now bound for the town below.

"Don't worry if you can't catch up! I'll land, eventually..." The rock person yelled back as Clemat struggled to catch his breath.

Clemat staggered, his body was weak, and his breath was getting increasingly shallow with every step. But with one last push, he leapt, aiming for the tail end of the dandelion. He reached out even though the distance was still too far to grab, and it was obvious that he wasn't going to make it.

The rock person quickly angled herself so the dandelion's stem would be lowered. Just enough for Clemat to grab on and pull himself up.

His weight throws the dandelion off balance. It dipped at first, but his struggles to hold himself up angled it in a way that caught a strong gust of wind. The dandelion spun itself high in the air while they both clung on as tightly as they could.

"... Th.... Thanks..." Clemat muttered as he slowly opened his eyes again "Woah!"

From this height, Clemat could see the rivers that cut through the town, the lush green grass that makes up its bed and the clusters of dandelions on the edge of it. As well as the mountain range that surrounded the town which was impossible to miss.

Even though it wasn't as huge as the ones on earth, it still towered over everything, blocking the view of the other side. There was also what looked like a cotton forest that sat in between it and the town.

The orange clouds bathed the land in an orange glow while the mountains and rivers shimmered with the light. The beauty of the valley captivated him.

Taking a glance behind them, he looked at the spot where he woke. The grassy plains extend to the ocean that stretches beyond the horizon. There was no sand, no edge of the water. Just grass, grass, grass then the ocean. It clicked for Clemat. The winds blowing them toward the town is a constant sea breeze.

"It's boring, isn't it? Can't wait to get out of this place." The rock person said. Breaking the calm silence.

"What are you talking about? This is amazing! Way better than a world of hay!" Clemat exclaimed, still gawking at the scenery. "I'm uh... I'm Clemat by the way."

"What's hay?"

"It's like dead, dried up grass. Not as soft as you'd think, and it gets everywhere."

"Grass doesn't dry up, are you okay? Did you get bonked too hard in the head? And uhm... I'm Pebbles."

Clemat didn't respond. He was too busy soaking it in as they slowly drifted towards the town.

Chapter Two

The pair landed on the eastern outskirts of town. Pebbles hopped down from the dandelion with a heavy thud. Clemat's legs wobbled as he stepped down, grabbing onto Pebbles for balance.

Pebbles was half his height and smooth all around. Similar to rocks by the lake that was perfect for skipping. When caught in the right light, a soft sparkle revealed itself.

"Here we are. Welcome to New Cottown." Pebbles said, stepping out from supporting Clemat.

"For the cotton forest behind it? Creative."

"Finally! Someone understands!"

Clemat started walking ahead of Pebbles, fascinated by the town just up ahead. The coconut houses were just in view, some were full coconut with a small base cut out for stability while others were half a coconut embedded in the ground.

"So, what's new about it?" Clemat asked, feeling somewhat like a tourist.

"NOTHING! THAT'S THE PROBLEM!" Pebbles said with her hands in the air while her feet dragged behind Clemat. "I would just love to be able to leave, explore the world beyond this. Maybe even survive on my own and find something new!"

"Then why don't you? Seems as easy as just getting up and leaving."

"Didn't you see me trying? Anyways, it's not that simple, there are just so many things I need to think about..." Pebbles sounded unsure as she progressed through that sentence.

Clemat didn't press further, they'd just met after all. He chugged along, slightly in front of Pebbles, excited to see the world he's been dropped into.

As they entered the town, Clemat noticed that there were no streets, but tiny paths lined with totems that glowed orange from the top. It emanated from the luminous orange cotton on it which was encased in a stalk-like material that looks to have come from the dandelion. Like a tiki streetlamp.

"Hey, Pebbles. How did you guys make the cotton glow?" Clemat asked as he came to a halt and just stared.

"We stuffed the clouds in them." Pebbles replied with an unenthusiastic tone.

"Wait... so the clouds above are actually glowing orange? And how did you even get them down?" Clemat continued, more confused than ever.

"Yes, they glow, we have light as long as we have clouds, if not we have these totems." Pebbles began to monologue, "If the clouds don't move and get too heavy, pieces of them will fall, so we put them in the cotton. Pretty basic stuff, but picking up the clouds is one of the worst chores ever..."

Clemat got excited and started moving again. He trailed further in front, giddy with every step. They passed by a few other rock people of different sizes. Most waving at  Pebbles but giving him a weird look when he came into view.

He was used to it by now.

They had a society of their own, a world that's different from his own, but feels familiar somehow. Some were talking amongst themselves, others used grass brooms to sweep the top of their coconut houses. One was balancing on a ladder next to a totem and fluffing the cotton while another rock person, the size of Pebbles, stood below, looking up expectantly.

Pebbles started to feel self-conscious with all the glances they were attracting. She knew everyone by name, they knew who she was too. And they knew what she was up to that afternoon. She needed to distract herself, to focus herself back on her goal and away from the doubt.

"Hey, can I ask you one question? How did you get here? And can you show me how to get out?"

"That's not one question, and..." He patted his jacket pocket to feel his notebook, "I'm not sure."

"Not sure how you got here or how to get out...?"

"Yes," Clemat replied, now he actively avoided Pebbles' gaze.

It wasn't as if Clemat was hiding anything from Pebbles. He could feel Pebbles slow down, could feel her thinking things through and could feel her sense of place. *I wish I knew too*, he thought while he kept moving forward, genuinely curious with his surroundings and pretending that Pebbles would just go along with it.

Pebbles' steps grew heavier, slower and eventually, they stopped. She was unsatisfied with his answer but could hear the sincerity in his voice. *Why is it so easy for you to just keep moving while I'm stuck here? Is it me?* She thought, reliving her most recent failure while admiring Clemat's forward momentum.

"PEBS! You are finally back! We saw you in the sky, are you ok?" A soothing voice called out from the right. It snapped them both out of their funk.

Clemat looked back, trying to find the source of the voice.

Three paths down to the right of Pebbles, two larger rock people stood in front of a coconut house. The one with the smooth voice waved her hands while walking towards them.

The second, gruffly looking, rock person trailed behind slowly. Those soft eyes locked on Clemat, holding his gaze before shifting to Pebbles too.

Pebbles hung her head low while she moved towards them. Clemat didn't let the gap widen too much before he followed.

"Yea I'm fine, the sea breeze kept blowing me back... I'll never get out..." Pebbles said sheepishly.

"Not this again..." said the rock with a soothing voice, though they sounded a little more annoyed this time.

"I found something though, or someone." Pebbles said, cutting them off and redirecting the subject to Clemat.

Clemat approached to find that even though the two rock people were larger than Pebbles, they were only as tall as his brow.

"Hey," he said, raising his right hand for a small wave.

"These are my parents!" Pebbles said proudly to Clemat, then turning to her parents "And yea, this is Clemat. A... I don't know what he is... he's nice though."

"Name's Marbles, nice to meet you!" Said the first rock person with a soothing voice.

"Rockford," said the second rock person right as he caught up to them. "Thanks for keeping Pebbs safe."

As soon as those words ended, the air around them seemed to have gone still. The wind blew as constant as ever but Clemat could feel the awkward tension rising. The four of them started walking back towards the house in silence, which only made the tension grow.

"Pebbles had things under control, I was just along for the ride," Clemat said a few steps in, to break the ice. "I'm a human by the way. What are you guys?"

Rockford grunted while Marbles lets the silence sit for a little before providing a reply. "We are Amphibolite. Seeing as we've never heard of what a human is, I guess it's safe to assume that we'd be foreign to you too."

Clemat nodded in agreement.

Before long, they arrived at the front of the house. It was a large coconut with the bottom third of it cut off. It sat on the grass, creating a dome shape with a cut-out door. In front of the house sat a totem light and a bench made out of stalks from a different plant. One that looks sturdier and more wood-like.

Marbles gestured, inviting Clemat into their home. He stepped in without hesitation while Marbles followed behind.

After they all headed into the house, Pebbles kicked around outside. She looked in the direction of the winds that furiously blew the grass and furs on the coconut house. Letting the familiar breeze brush up against her face.

Rockford stood at the door, watching his daughter. He felt a mixture of pride and frustration. Conflicting emotions were cut short when Pebbles turned around to look at him.

"Come on in now, youngin'. Time to be a good host.

<u>Chapter Three</u>

Inside the coconut house was surprisingly spacious. There were tiny stools made up of dandelion stalks. A little coffee table made from the same material as the bench outside. There were no other rooms, no beds, no washrooms, just a one-room coconut igloo.

Clemat noticed that the floor was still grass, it just continued from outside in. The place was also lit up with cotton stuffed cloud lights hung up with blades of grass that were strung into a rope. The curved walls were decorated with little trinkets made out of grass and or cotton that were woven together.

Marbles noticed that Clemat was studying the trinkets on the wall. They walked over carefully to not startle him.

"Those were made by Pebbs and I. Pebbs gets so attached to them that we could never throw them out." Marbles said, "Would love to barter them at the market, but Pebbs would get so self-conscious."

"They look great! I'd get them." Clemat replied. "Looks like art does exist everywhere huh?"

"What are you guys chatting about?" Pebbles said as she walked in. Rockford followed closely behind. She quickly noticed that they were standing in front of the trinket wall and continued, "Those are nothing... pish... I could have made them better."

Clemat asked about how they were made and how the grass is so strong that it can be tied into a rope. He was curious as to why the grass doesn't dry out and lose its strength once it's been plucked from the ground.

Marbles and Pebbles explained enthusiastically as Rockford walked past them to take his place on one of the small stools.

"What were you doing on those dandelions again?" Rockford asked, cutting off the previous conversation. "What do you plan to do if you DO manage to get past the sea breeze? Just float in the middle of the ocean?"

"Are we really doing this now?" Pebbles retorted. "What happened to 'be a good host'?"

Rockford maintained his stern but soft gaze on Pebbles. The room fell back into silence, but it wasn't uncomfortable this time. Clemat felt the concern and the worry that emanated from her parents.

Marbles took a seat on the stool beside Rockford. Their attention now fully on Pebbles who, on the other hand, was super uncomfortable, shooting looks back at Clemat.

Help me... she mouthed to Clemat. Clemat awkwardly walked up next to the parents and took a seat on the final stool. Pebbles sighed. Not impressed but understood.

"So, were you just going to float there?" Rockford pressed again.

Pebbles sat on the grassy floor in front of them, now forming a little circle between the four of them.

"Well, I was planning on flying high enough to see if there was anything other than water out there..." she said softly.

"What if you fell? We can't float." Marbles asked.

"I wouldn't have fallen." Pebbles replied, agitation coming through in her voice. "Tell them, Clemat!"

"So... What do you guys eat around here..." Clemat said, desperately trying to change the subject.

He wanted to help Pebbles but didn't want to lie. Rockford and Marbles might have sounded like they were disappointed and discouraging, but their body language didn't show it. To Clemat, this felt more like a review than an interrogation.

"Eat?" Pebbles inquired, totally on board with the plan.

"You guys don't need to eat? Um... then if you don't mind, I need to." Clemat said as he took out an energy bar from his pocket and tore it open. "It's a human thing. Really sorry, I need to do this, to y'know..."

The three of them looked at him curiously as he bit into it.

"...Stay alive?" He continued with a mouth full of food.

Rockford grunted.

They waited for him to swallow his first bite before Marbles jumped in. "Clemat, you look like someone well-travelled. How do you like this place?"

Pebbles was relieved that Marbles took the bait.

"Well from what I've seen... It's pretty great! Would love to explore a little more of it. Everything's so soft and cosy..."

"And super boring..." Pebbles mumbled.

Rockford grunted.

"Pebbs." Marbles said, trying to stop her.

"You know I'm right! One day I'll leave!" Pebbles fell back into the previous conversation without knowing it. Her mind was still occupied with her failed attempt that afternoon. "One day I'll... I'll..."

"Please... we have been here for generations..." Marbles continued, "You'll need to..."

"By force? We are trapped!" Pebbles exclaimed. She was frustrated but didn't raise her voice. "We can't leave by sea because we can't float. Can't leave by air because of the breeze while the mountains and forest block off the other way!"

"Enough, youngin." Rockford voiced up.

"We aren't trapped..." Marbles continued, "It's just that..."

"Just what? You don't trust me? You don't trust that I'll be able to survive on my own?"

"Enough," Rockford said again.

"Um..." Clemat interjected, breaking the tension. "Has anyone actually left before?"

"Of course, n.." Pebbles answered quickly.

"Yes," Rockford said, turning to Clemat.

"Ford..." Marbles sighed. "Yes, some left before. A long time ago, and we've never heard back from them. We don't even know if they made it out of the forest or up the mountain. It's scary, not knowing if they are alright..."

"So, why don't you just go?" Clemat said, turning to Pebbles. "And keep in contact, let them know you are okay?"

"What? How?"

"It's dangerous, not knowing if you are alright, it worries us that..." Rockford said as he looked at Marbles then turned to Pebbles. Pebbles sat there quietly, she looked like she was losing steam.

Clemat noticed it too. The vigour that Pebbles was arguing with quickly dissipated with each passing word. Her shoulders slumped as she absently gazed at the ground.

"You just need to know that Pebbles is fine right?" He turned to the parents. Clemat then put his hands on her shoulders and gave a light nod to her parents, "We will figure something out. Don't you worry!"

"Send us a signal," Rockford said. "Send us a signal using the cloud lights when you get to the top of the mountain. That way we'll know you are okay."

"That... is possible..." Pebbles perked back up though her voice still shook.

"What are you worried about? I'll be going along with you!" Clemat jumped in, trying to hype her back up. "Wanted to explore this place more anyways."

"But... but... if we don't see the signal after three days, we are going out there to get you!" Marbles adding a new clause. "Deal?"

"Okay! Deal!" Pebbles replied, all excited again.

"Not so fast youngin," Rockford says calmly. "We need you to do something before we are fully sold."

"A test?" Pebbles asked, shoulders slumped down again, this time a little more annoyed. It was as if this was not too uncommon for her parents.

They stared intently at Rockford. Clemat felt excitement building up in him while he turned to see Pebbles crack a nervous smile.

"More of a proof of commitment." Rockford said before turning to Clemat "from the both of you."

Chapter Four

The four of them walked through the town, Pebbles and Rockford a couple of feet ahead of Clemat and Marbles. Pebbles had a little pouch on her. It was weaved out of grass and filled with what she thought was needed to complete the tasks.

"Is the forest that dangerous?" Clemat asked.

"It's less the forest that I'm worried about, it's what's after." Marbles said, "Yes, it's dangerous, but so is every other route out of here."

"Have you guys tried?"

25

"Different rocks want different things," Marbles said with a smile, though their eyes told a different story. "We are content with where we are, every parent just wants their child to have an easy life."

Clemat didn't answer, he couldn't. The last memories he had with his parents were unrealistically hazy. Though the thought of them formed a pit in his stomach.

Soon, they arrived at their destination. The Dandelion Grove loomed over them. The stalks were tall with clusters of dandelion seeds, much like the ones Clemat and Pebbles rode in on, that populated the top of them.

The shorter stalks have a green tinge while the mature ones developed a darker colour. Clemat could see that these were used as the material for some of the furniture in the house and around town. Many of the taller stalks have a ladder leaning on them, though it doesn't reach the top.

A couple of rock people waved to Rockford and nodded at Marbles as they passed. They were hauling a bundle of harvested stalks behind them.

"Thought it was your day off Ford?" One of them said jokingly, then turning to Pebbles "Here to show him the ropes?"

Rockford grunted while Pebbles gave an awkward smile. Rockford colleagues got a glimpse of Clemat and leaned away from him.

"Thanks for watching her climb to the top of these things without letting me know," Rockford said, matching their joking tone in an attempt to change the subject.

"At least the kid's taking somewhat of an interest!" They said while they continued with their work.

Once they were out of earshot, Rockford turned to Clemat and Pebbles.

"So, you understand your task?"

The both of them nodded, but Marbles chimed in again "Find the Forever Stalk and leave your mark."

"Cool, let's go," Clemat said as he turned to walk into the Dandelion Grove. Pebbles kicked around back for a couple of seconds, staring back at her parents, seeming unsure of herself.

Rockford gave Pebbles a stern look and a gentle nod, the one only a father can. Clemat came back and pulled Pebbles in behind him. " I can't find the way on my own, let's go!"

" I can't either, I don't know where the Forever Stalk is." Pebbles replied as they wandered deeper in and further away from her parents.

"What is that anyway?" Clemat said without slowing down. "Is it like that one stalk you guys never cut down?"

"That's exactly it. This is the test all dandelion harvesters get when they're at the end of their apprenticeship." Pebbles slowed down even more as she provided exposition. "But I'm not done with my apprenticeship yet, in fact, I'm only a couple of months in."

The deeper they got in; the density of dandelion stalks increased. Clemat noticed that the ones without a ladder had divots carved in as a way to climb them.

The orange clouds above provided enough light, though the colour is darker than before. The grassy ground was covered with shadows cast from above, forming a pattern with pockets of dark orange light shining through.

Though night-time was approaching, Pebbles didn't seem to worry, as if she's been through this before. The height and sizes vary but one thing stayed consistent.

"The stalks," Clemat pointed out. "The taller stalks, they are all a lot thicker than the ones before. So, if we just follow the pattern..."

"We should be brought to the Forever Stalk!" Pebbles jumped up with joy.

Soon, they were walking at full speed, eyes peeled on the difference between the stalks. Pebbles used her pouch as a measuring tool while she handed a braided trinket to Clemat to do the same. The trinket was woven from grass, braided with 3 weaves and had a loop at the top. Clemat uncoiled it so that it was as its maximum length for the job.

The both of them got deeper and deeper, but there was no sign of the Forever Stalk. Eventually, they got to the end of the grove and faced the ocean beyond them. Ocean water pushed and pulled up to the land's edge, wetting the grass that's brave enough to make contact.

"Are you sure this thing exists?" Clemat asked, "It's not just something that they get the newbies to do as a prank, right?"

Pebbles hesitated before answering "It exists. It's the largest stalk in the land, the original one, or at least that's what everyone says."

The both of them stared out at the ocean, the sea breeze tussling Clemat's hair and covering their faces with its comforting embrace. He bent down, stuck his finger in the ocean and put it in his mouth.

"I should have paid more attention…" Pebbles said while Clemat stuck out his tongue at how salty the water was. "Always thought this was just my parents' way of distracting me from exploring."

"It probably is." Clemat said. "Come on, let's head back in, we are close, I can feel it."

Pebbles stood there, motionless. She stared out at the horizon, wondering if this was all worth it. Maybe this was the place she belonged after all. This was her life, her community. Why else would her parents want her to leave her mark on the Forever Stalk if not to tell her that this is where she belongs, now and always.

Clemat put his hand on her smooth glistening head. "Hey, think about it. We are not completely off base. We should be close since the stalks at the end are a lot thicker than the ones at the front. Another thing is that this stalk since it's so special, should be protected right?"

Pebbles snapped out of her trance as Clemat continued his deduction. "So that means there shouldn't be that many other stalks around it. I'm not sure how plants here work, but back home, if you cut down too many around that one tree, it will also start to wilt and die. Especially if that's supposed to be the 'Mother Stalk' or something like that."

"That makes sense." Pebbles responded. "We then just need to observe our surroundings a little more than just the thickness of the stalks."

"Exactly! We were stuck in a tunnel-vision that we must've passed it somewhere."

The pair headed back into the grove once again and started observing the plantation as a whole and not just each dandelion stalk individually. As they got deeper to the centre, they noticed that the gaps between the stalks grew wider as well. Excited, they ran, closer and closer to the centre until they reached it.

The Forever Stalk.

It was taller than any other around it. The stalk had a dark brown colour to it, showing its age. While the others around the Forever Stalk were arranged in almost a circle, giving it an air of grandiose. This also caused there to be nothing obstructing the dark orange clouds from shining through, bathing it in its spotlight. Near the top of the stalk, just below the dandelion puff were a bunch of names carved in by the harvesters before them.

Near the bottom of the rows, they could see Rockford's name carved in.

"Alright, time to leave your mark."

Pebbles took out a couple of wood pieces from her pack, ready to chisel some grab holds to climb up. She walked up to the base of the stalk and stood there.

"What happened?"

"I can't damage the Forever Stalk," she said. "Take a look, all these rocks had their names carved in, but there are no holds leading up to them."

"Isn't carving your name already damaging the stalk? Don't think any of the ladders around are even remotely tall enough to reach that specific area."

They both sat there for a bit, trying to figure out a way through this. The sky was getting darker above them. Before long, Rockford and Marbles appeared behind them.

"Why are you guys just sitting here?" Marbles asked. They walked up to Pebbles.

31

Pebbles stayed still while Clemat looked back at them. He shook his head and raised his hand a little, signalling them to give them space

"We can't damage the stalk, and the ladders around aren't tall enough," Clemat replied. Rockford grunted and kept his eyes peeled on his daughter.

"I…" Pebbles said softly, without looking back at her parents "I just need to leave my mark, right?"

Rockford grunted.

"Clem, can you pass me the trinket?"

"Yea, it's all unravelled." Clemat gave her the unwoven grass trinket.

"No worries, I got an idea," Pebble said, finally turning back, with a smile on her face. She took a couple of moments to weave it back together, the three braids overlapped each other again like they were meant to be.

Clemat tried to study the process, but he was quickly lost in all the intricate steps that was second nature to Pebbles. The bottom of the trinket was left flowing with 3 loose ends while the top had a tight loop to head it.

Pebbles then started throwing the trinket at the Forever Stalk, over and over again. Clemat understood what Pebbles was trying to do. He quickly ran to grab a nearby ladder and held it as straight as possible.

"P," he called out to her, waiting for her to look back down at him. "I got you."

"Okay." Pebbles replied.

As Clemat struggled to keep the ladder stable, Pebbles climbed to the top of it. Once at the top, she took a deep breath, twirled the trinket around her arm and let it go just at the right time. It flew gracefully through the air, smacked onto the Forever Stalk, and slid down its surface.

The trinket fell on the ground a couple times. After each attempt, Pebbles would climb down to retrieve it and try again. Clemat held the ladder up vertically as steady as he could, pausing to stretch whenever they needed to reset.

After what felt like the hundredth attempt, the trinket soared gracefully through the air. Pebbles adjusted her trajectory enough times. She was ready for it to work. Once again, the trinket smacked on the stalk and slid down.

The four of them looked on in anticipation, not sure what to expect.

The trinket slid down the woody stalk, but before it could hit the ground, the loop caught itself in a scab and clung to it tightly. Pebbles and Clemat cheered.

"Hey, come down! I can't hold you up any longer!" He said with a cheeky grin.

Pebbles took a few steps down the ladder before stepping off it and slid down into his embrace. They both continued to cheer. The parents stood behind them, smiling.

After celebrations died down, they turned back to marvel at accomplishing the task.

"It's time." Rockford whispered to Marbles who had a soft smile and tears hanging from their eyes.

The trinket caught itself on the K of a harvester named Rockford.

Chapter Five

Back home, Pebbles was ecstatic. She recounted their trial and the conclusion she came to as she and Marbles were waving together a larger bag with the grass around them.

Clemat was happy for Pebbles, he sat on the grass and observed the family. Their dynamic was familiar to him though he couldn't quite put his finger on it. He noticed Pebbles hopping around Marbles, doing more acting than weaving while Marbles slowed down to listen to their daughter. He could see that they were putting on a proud smile, but their eyes were also watering.

Rockford was quiet, he sat on the opposite side of the house, close to his family. He was so still that Clemat almost didn't notice him there. The parents had their eyes locked on Pebbles the entire night. Clemat was almost certain that they were soaking in every last bit of her.

The idea of not knowing if your child was going to return must be a scary one. He thought.

After dark, the rocks hugged themselves and lowered their whole bodies to the ground, freezing like a statue. A small circle of light formed on the grass under and around them. It was as if they are recharging with the nutrients from the earth. The circumference around Pebbles was smaller but brighter than the parents.

Clemat shuffled around on the grassy ground but couldn't sleep. He noticed Rockford getting up quietly. Curious, he followed Rockford to the bench outside the coconut house. The sky was dark, almost pitch black. It was only dimly illuminated by the large mass of dark and dirty orange clouds.

"Can't sleep?" Clemat asked.

"Sorry about before. Wanted to be a good host, but my temper got the best of me." Rockford grunted before answering.

"Don't worry about it. I understand."

They sat in silence for a while, just looking up at the night sky. No clouds directly above them. But the breeze carried a huge one in from the north.

"I know that trial wasn't really meant for me," Clemat said again.

Rockford grunted and adjusted himself on the bench. He stretched his arms back and rested them to his side.

"Asked Marbles this on the way back" He said while they stared out at the night sky. Clemat unsure if he was actively avoiding his gaze. "If we are bad parents for wanting to keep out daughter safe. To give her the life that we have."

Clemat didn't respond. It felt like he has heard or have been told this before from someone close to him. Though he couldn't put his finger on it.

He quickly brushed it aside thinking that this was just a universal thing that every parent would face and project onto their children.

"Wondered if we were being reasonable for wanting her to have an easy life." Rockford continued "Or were we just stopping her from reaching to the top of that ladder."

"I've been to many places... willingly or not. I'll take care of Pebbles for as long as I'm able to. Don't worry."

There was no response for a while as they sat there in the quiet. Only letting the wind whisper in their ears.

"Pebbles will be fine. No need to trouble you there. Capable and resourceful, that one is. Able to move universes if attempted. The way she accomplished the Harvester's Trial is proof enough of that." Rockford said proudly before his toned changed, "Just wish Pebbles would believe that too…"

"Yea…" Clemat answered out of formality.

"Thought making her an apprentice would give her purpose, confidence… and options" Rockford explained. "We know she sees it differently; it has always been hard to budge a rock when they've made up their mind about something."

The large cloud mass hung over their heads now and the sky lit up orange again. But this time with a dark and moody orange tinge before it started to fall. Small pieces of clouds floated down gently, like large pieces of snow.

"It's always hard on parents to see their child leave. Seeing your child doubt themselves makes it even tougher." Rockford said as he stood up. "Having confidence in yourself is only step one. Though, it plays such an important role in the entire narrative that it's impossible to ignore."

Clemat reflected on those words. He now fully understood that the parents were never against Pebbles following her dreams. They were afraid like any parent would, and Pebbles' bouts of self-doubt weren't helping.

"Let's head in."

"I'll... I'll catch up with you," Clemat said.

Rockford entered the house as Clemat sat there alone on the bench. He watched them fall. Little orbs of light floating down around him.

"Self-confidence huh?" Clemat whispered, patting the notebook in his jacket's pocket. "Most times, the universe doesn't care. It just wisps you to wherever it wants you to be.

He lifted his hands to catch a falling cloud. One fairly large piece landed on his palms, illuminating it with an orange glow, a glow brighter than the gloomy mass above. He stared at it for a while before pocketing it and walking back into the house for the night.

As he closed the door, the clouds continued to fall, landing on the grass, roof, and all around.

****

Early the next morning, Clemat paced around the house, anxious to get going. As the Rocks woke up, he noticed that the lights below them recede into the bottom of their forms. Their legs extend to standing and their arms stretched out. It looked as if a gargoyle came to life for the first time. The patches of grass they were on, oddly enough, don't have print on them.

Clemat stared for a bit, trying to piece together what he just witnessed. He squinted his eyes and focused on the grass beneath them. It was as if nothing had been putting pressure on it all night.

"Good! You're awake! Let's go!" Clemat said after regaining his composure.

"How long have you been up?" Pebbles replied, groggy and unimpressed.

"Long enough to take a walk around town. Man, you guys sleep in." Clemat said, "Only a couple of your neighbours were awake, said they were heading out for the harvest. But they were not going to the Dandelion Grove?"

"Oh, that must be Cliff and Grav. They must be headed to harvest some cotton from the outskirts of the forest." Marbles chimed in. "The Cotton Harvesters start their days earlier because of the dangers of the forest, compared to the Dandelion Harvesters anyways."

As they were chatting, Rockford already made his way outside while Marbles packed more cloud lights from the night before into the bag made out of weaved grass.

"What are you doing? I can pack for myself..." Pebbles said sheepishly.

"Just wanted to help you get a head start. Clemat's already ready to go."

Pebbles walked over and helped finish the packing. They mainly packed a large piece of cotton wrapped around clusters of fallen, glowing clouds and a bunch of grass. Slowly filling up her pack with the same material at the top of the light totems that lined the streets. Clemat just stared at these rock people as it looked like they stuffed cotton and grass into a bag made of grass.

Soon, they were all standing outside the house, Clemat and Pebbles facing the parents.

"You remember the goal?" Marbles asked.

"Yea, get to the top of the mountain in three days and signal back to show that I'm ok and can handle it." Pebbles replied with a soft, worried smile.

"If not, we are coming to get you," Rockford grunted.

"Just trust me! I'll be fine..." Pebbles was trying to put up a brave front, but second thoughts crept in as she kept her eyes on her parents, her home and the place she grew up in.

"Don't worry youngin," Rockford said, in a deep and reassuring voice as Marbles held his hand and leaned in. "You've left your mark on this place. No matter how far you go. You will always have somewhere you belong."

Pebbles turned her head in the direction of the Dandelion Grove. She choked up a little but held it back as best she could.

Clemat stood slightly behind Pebbles. He felt the bond between this family, and he felt regret. "Great! Thanks for having me, and let's go, Pebbles!" He said as he turned to leave, shoving those feelings aside.

"Uh wait... it feels like I forgot something."

"Come on, we will be fine. Let's go!"

"Okay... I guess this is it." Pebbles said, pausing a little before running into her parent's arms for a hug.

"Take care, we will be in contact in three days," Marbles said as they hug their daughter tight.

Rockford grunted, but it's noticeably different this time. More choked up than a grunt.

Clemat stopped in his tracks. He caught himself staring again and looked away quickly. He gave a little smile and looked up at the orange lit sky again.

"Please, just let me stay here for more than three days…" He whispered to himself. "Please."

"Who are you talking to, weirdo?" Pebbles said as she gave him a little jab on his arm. It was surprisingly painful coming from a small rock fist.

"Anyone that would hear me." He said with a smile while rubbing his sore arm.

Pebbles looked at him, confused.

"Alright, you ready?" Clemat asked, hyping things up. "Let's get to it!"

Chapter Six

Everyone they come across town waved to Pebbles. Once again, Pebbles slowed down, second-guessing the decision. It seemed like everything in her mind told her not to do it. Though she knew she wouldn't be satisfied if she didn't at least try.

"Do you think… they know that they're actually saying bye…"

"What do you think is on the other side of that mountain?" Clemat said while patting her back. He was trying to change the subject. Knowing full well that leaving is never easy but didn't want to cloud her judgement in case this wasn't what she wanted after all.

"I don't know…" Pebbles replied interest piqued once again. "Maybe a small, tiny ocean that is long instead of wide?"

"You mean river?" Clemat laughed. "Yea that'll be amazing, we can just ride the stream and see where it takes you!"

"All the way to the edge of the world!"

Their fantasies came to a halt when they arrived at the entrance to the forest.

"So those are cotton trees?" Clemat asked as they approached.

The cotton trees were not exactly trees, they were more like large clusters of cotton connected by branches to the ground. Basically, white cotton candy with wooden holding sticks that grow from the earth.

"Hey! Pebbles!" A Rock Person stood on top of a ladder and waved as they passed him. The ladder was leaning up against a cotton tree while a basket filled with cotton sat at the base.

Pebbles waved back as they stepped foot into the forest. Clemat remembered them from his walk this morning. Putting together that this must be Cliff, the Cotton Harvester.

Cliff got off his ladder and ran toward them, tipping over his basket of harvested cotton. Cliff was slightly taller than

Rockford but not as stout. His head was longer as well, giving him more of a scholarly look if glasses existed in this universe.

"What are you doing?! You can't go in there!" Cliff said in a panic.

"Huh? Why not?" Clemat asked, wondering who gave him the authority.

Grav slowly came up behind Cliff and stood behind quietly. Grav was about the same size as Pebbles and looked to be Cliff's child.

"Well, stranger," Cliff retorted "Pebbles should have told you, that a Gramoglogen is living there…"

"A what?"

"It's just a creature that lives in there, we've never seen it, but we hear its bleats once in a while." Pebbles said dismissively.

"I've seen it alright! It's huge!" Cliff started going off, slightly hysterical. "Has four large branches growing out of its head and if it sees you, it'll charge towards you with all its might, knocking you over and dragging you away… They say it changes the trees in the forest so you can never get out…."

Grav was startled and hid behind Cliff.

"So, it's like a four-horned horned demon?" Clemat asked further.

"A demon? I don't know what that is, but it sounds like a better name than the Gramoglogen." Cliff answered.

"Well, thanks for the warning, let's go P."

"No! I won't let you through, it's too dangerous!" Cliff turned his attention to Pebbles. "Did your parents allow this? It's not another one of your experiments again, is it?"

"I was close to flying out at that time..." Pebbles was annoyed but didn't know how to proceed. "And yea, my parents gave the okay... They never seemed to believe it... at least one of them didn't..."

Pebbles paused.

"...But maybe we should think about it... Maybe that's why my parents were afraid of me leaving..."

"Don't worry, I'm here to help," Clemat reassured her. "It's just a straight shot to the end, right? There's nothing to worry about, Let's get going already."

Cliff sighed with frustration. Clemat, feeling the cold shoulder from Cliff, leaned into helping Pebbles gain confidence.

"Okay, so how did you escape being seen by the demon?" Clemat continued, directing his question at Cliff.

"I was lucky that it didn't see me, I spotted it from afar, heard it bleating and I ran out as fast as I could. Should have listened during my apprenticeship." He said, turning to Grav at the mention of his apprenticeship. "Now we just harvest cotton from the entrance, which is way more than we need anyway!"

Cliff seemed proud of the situation almost. Pebbles sat down, staring at the grass.

"Hey, you want to do this right?" Clemat chimed in again. "So, let's do this... waiting here won't help you see the world."

He tried to phrase it gently, but his impatience was coming through.

"Okay... We will get to the end and up that mountain..." Pebbles responded slowly. "But we need a plan, just in case the Gramoglogen is real and tries to change the forest..."

Pebbles peeled off a small light cloud from her bag and walked over to Cliff's tipped over the basket.

"Mind if I take one Cliff? Wanna conserve the ones in my bag for later..."

They all look at Pebbles, curious.

"Conserve them for what?" Cliff asked, still giving off scared dad energy.

Pebbles ignored Cliff's question while stuffing the lighted cloud into a piece of cotton. Once the clouds were in, the cotton glowed a soft light orange, Pebbles then massaged the top of the cotton to seal it up. She then walked over to the entrance of the forest and started digging. Before long, there was a small hole in the ground in which she planted the cotton halfway in.

"If the Gramoglogen can move the trees, then we just need a signal to know that we are going in a straight line." The others looked on as Pebbles monologues the plan while she dug the hole. "By planting the lighted pieces of cotton halfway into the ground, it'll become like…"

"Like a runway! You're a genius P!" Clemat exclaimed. "Now we can always tell if we are going in a straight line just by looking back."

"Also, we can retrace our steps if we happen to make a wrong turn and for the others to find us if we do get lost." Pebbles said with a smile. "So, Cliff? What do you think?"

Cliff stood there silently with his both hands on his hips. He contemplated while Grav shuffled closer to the planted cotton light, impressed. Grav padded down the sides of the planted cotton to give it more security. Though it didn't really do much, he looked back seeking approval from the others.

"My parents gave us three days. If I don't signal them from the top of the mountain by then, you guys can use the trail to find us."

"No… no… We will get there in three days and this runway can help you guys, maybe expand your town or something." Clemat chimed in.

The both of them stood there quietly as Cliff continued to contemplate. He made eye contact with Clemat and quickly turned to Pebbles.

Something about Pebbles was different to him. He wasn't sure if it was because of Clemat's presence or perhaps it's because of her parents' permission.

"Okay... If your parents are fine with it, then I should just trust their confidence." Cliff said to Pebbles, still a little hesitant.

"You can trust me too."

"Yes... yes, of course, I do." Cliff said, a little stunned. "Good luck to the both of you."

Chapter Seven

A couple of hours after entering the forest, the two settled into a routine. Clemat held onto the bag, making the cloud light, and tossed it back to Pebbles who dug the holes and planted them in the ground.

"Clem, look!" Pebbles called out, taking a break from planting.

Clemat turned around to see Pebbles rubbing the cotton furiously on her head.

"What are you…"

Small strands of static developed, and the cotton stuck fast to Pebbles' head. Clemat rushed back to examine it closer. He tried to pull on it to test its integrity. It held tight to her head, but before long, the charge depleted, and it fell off on its own. It reminded him of rubbing socks on the carpet.

"Cool right? Ha-ha, used to do this a bunch when I was little." Pebbles exclaimed, excited. "I and the other kids would run around attracting more cotton to us that we turned into cotton stones!"

The more childish side of Pebbles brought a smile to Clemat's face. He could imagine Pebbles, Grav and the other kids eventually becoming huge cotton balls themselves. He rubbed a new piece of cotton on Pebbles and pull it off after, but it stuck on hard.

"That's so cool! Does it work for me?"

He started rubbing the cotton on his hair. It didn't stick, but there was enough static to point it high in the air. Not long after his attempt, the second piece of cotton fell off Pebbles on its own.

They both laughed, enjoying their journey and each other's company.

After a few rounds of these goofs and getting to know each other better, not stopping their trek in the process, they managed to get quite a way deep into the forest. Clemat found Pebbles' stories fascinating, her childhood was simple, boring, some might even say privileged. However, it didn't stop her from wanting more, wanting to escape that weighted security blanket.

Pebbles was equally amused and confused by Clemat. He was so foreign yet so familiar. He couldn't tell her much of the previous worlds, aside the one with dead grass and a vague memory of the one before it. That felt odd, but at the same time, she could tell he wasn't hiding anything.

Though the further in they got they heavier the sense of unease. There had been a constant howling of the winds which didn't seem natural throughout their long trek.

It got increasingly obvious over time. The longer they were in there, the more they noticed a strange force that shifted the cotton on the trees, so much so that it felt like they were moving.

"What was that?" Pebbles asked, halting their conversation with her worry.

Pattering sounds developed around them that grew louder with each passing moment. It sounded like the pattering of horses running at full speed, of their hooves hitting the gravel. It also seemed to increase in speed the faster the duo moved. The entire cotton trees also gave the impression that they were beginning to move shift and not just the top with the wind.

"It's the demo...." Clemat muttered.

"GRAMOGLOGEN!"

The both of them stood there, frozen. Pebbles a few feet behind Clemat. The patterning was getting so loud that it started to drown out the sounds around them. At this point, it is clear that there wasn't just one creature but a herd.

As the pattering of hooves got louder, they noticed that the trees were also now moving circularly around them. Increasing in speed gradually, trapping them in a vortex. The loud sounds followed the pattern of the swirling trees, it spiralled around them, drowning them in a sea of audible and visual confusion.

Pebbles crouched on the ground in fear with a couple of cotton lights hugged tight to her chest. She was shaking, looking down at her feet and breathing heavily.

A loud mixture between an elk's bleat and wolf's howl cut through all the noise, shocking them from their trance.

"Let's move! We can't let them surround us!" Clemat shouted back at Pebbles.

He started running with the bag on him. He didn't look back and fully expected Pebbles to follow.

But Pebbles didn't.

The sound was so overwhelming that they couldn't hear and eventually lost each other in the confusion. As Clemat got further and further away, so did the pattering sounds and the moving trees.

Soon, there were only the usual sounds of the winds remaining. Bringing everything back to a sense of calm. A sense of security.

Though it wasn't. Clemat was nowhere in sight and Pebbles was alone, still crouching on the ground. Her head was still down, eyes now shut, clutching onto the cloud lights as tightly as she could.

Chapter Eight

Clemat kept running, his breath catching up to him. The faster he tried to go, the more the trees kept swirling and turning around him. He was also started feeling unwell, vision doubled and tripping over himself a few times in the process.

"What do we do P?" He shouted back, barely able to hear himself over the noise. "They seem to be closing in and I'm getting really... really dizzy."

He stopped, knowing the dangers of doing so, he stopped. "P?"

He looked around him and stumbled. He managed to catch himself before falling but could barely hold in his urge to gag. The swirling started to slow as he did. Clemat took a little while to regain his composure, stood upright again and turned backed, hoping to find Pebbles there.

Thought it was as he feared. Pebbles is nowhere to be found.

"You've got to be kidding me!" Clemat began to pace, back and forth.

"P! PEBBLES!"

He was panting hard from the run, frustrated that Pebbles wasn't with him and afraid about what might be around him. He paced faster as he tried to calm himself down.

"Oh gosh, did Pebbles get eaten? No, no... I'm sure... no..."

The faster he paced, and the louder he complained, the louder the pattering became. It was now also interjected with the occasional bleats and howls, confirming to Clemat that it was a creature behind this and not some weird magic. He looked around him and saw the swirling begin to pick up speed again.

He quickly hid behind the closest tree, hoping that'll do something. Eventually, the swirling stopped, and the forest returned to its usual quiet.

"So, the tree works, that's good to know..." he said quietly to himself. "Ok, if I get back to where we were planting the lights, Pebbles should still be there. No, Pebbles will still be there!"

He hyped himself up and started running back, hoping to spot the lights soon. He made sure to look around in case the trees did move.

Not even a few steps in, the swirling and patterning returned. He quickly ducked behind a tree again, causing the swirling to slow and eventually phase-out. He sat down and was left with the quiet again, but his panting didn't slow.

Clemat popped his head out from the right of the tree, hoping to spot the creature. Nothing. It was calm. As he shifted to the left, his hands bumped into a cluster of stone shards on the ground. Though they were darker in colour, they had the familiar glimmer that Pebbles had.

He quickly hopped back. His breath got shallower, more driven by fear than exhaustion. He looked around, trying to find out if there were any more.

Beyond his breath, he heard a series of bleats and howls. His eyes darted all around him, sweat hanging from his frilled-up brow. He clutched tightly onto the bag straps, preparing for something to rear its head.

Clemat got up and walked slowly again, gradually picking up speed. All he could think about was how he needed to get back to Pebbles. As his speed increased, so did the demon.

Eventually, the swirling got so bad that he hid behind another tree until it went away.

"Great... this... is going to take a while."

Chapter Nine

Pebbles crouched there, she slowly opened her eyes and examined the three cloud lights left on the ground. The world around her was silent and still.

Looking around, she couldn't spot Clemat or any other creatures nearby. She took deep breaths in an attempt to calm herself, but her body kept on shaking.

Should I plant them? Move forward a little? She thought as she stood up. *Maybe I'll meet Clemat if I just move forward a little.*

Slowly, she stood up and walked back slow to the previous light and started the planting process again. Though her legs were trembling, she remembered the routine and focused on it as hard as she could.

First, Pebbles calculated the distance to where the next light should be planted, fifty paces. Then she steadily moved towards the direction she was before, counting each step out loud as she did. From here, she could tell that she was about twenty paces from where she was separated from Clemat.

During the little counting procedure, Pebbles heard a little pattering of hooves around her. It was distant, far enough that it could have been missed if Pebbles was not on high alert. The trees in the distance swirled as well, albeit incredibly slowly.

Pebbles froze, looking around to make sure nothing dangerous was approaching. Eventually, the sounds stopped, and the forest grew quiet again. All that's left was the sound of her remaining steps and the gentle wind.

Once she was sure everything was calm again, she sat down. Dug the hole with her hands and planted the light.

This repeated for the second light, the swirling and all. But Pebbles pauses midway through digging.

"This isn't right though, should I go back to the town for help?" She doubted. "No, if Clemat was eaten, he would have screamed. He must still be alive... he must be..."

Pebbles sat there next to the hole; tears formed. She tried to hold them back and continued to dig. She counted each movement, desperately trying to keep her mind of the worst. Even so, she was fighting a losing battle.

As she dug, tears fell on her hands and the ground in front of her. She failed to keep it back, just like she failed to make a decision and to move. The world felt so empty, it's so quiet and Pebbles felt helpless.

Is this... She thought before the rest of the words escaped her mouth. "Is this all I can do? Aren't I supposed to be capable of more?"

Without realizing it, the hole was so deep that Pebbles could fit in it. Pebbles paused, looking forward to seeing if Clemat was coming back. Then she looked back, wishing Rockford and Marbles would miraculously show up. That they would be there to greet her with a warm hug and a guiding hand home.

There was nothing but the planted lights before and the surrounding silence.

"Ok, no... I can't rush this." She mumbled to herself. "I can do this; I just need to slow down. I just need time to think..."

Pebbles got into the hole, hoping that it could provide a safe enough place to collect her thoughts. Clutching the two remaining cloud lights close to her chest, the dark little hole gave off a faint glow.

The glow was made brighter as lights appeared on the ground below her as when she sleeps. The clouds above faded away, causing the sky to darken as night falls over the land

<u>Chapter Ten</u>

Night-time arrived, the clouds above were largely absent, making way for the dark purple sky behind it. The forest would have been pitch black if not for the cloud lights planted.

Pebbles heard a soft thud next to the hole that she put herself in. But she stayed still, afraid of what might be waiting above. Pebbles shifted a little to remain comfortable while still being cautious to not draw too much attention from whatever waited for her above ground.

It didn't work.

There were two light taps on the top of her head. The only part that was slightly sticking out of the ground. The taps repeated getting a little faster with each interval.

Pebbles couldn't move. Her body was still frozen.

Suddenly, Pebbles felt something soft rubbing on top of her head. Back and forth, slowly and methodically. Gradually, the rub got more intense and sporadic.

"Cotton?" Pebbles whispered to herself.

Static began to develop, and the cotton stuck to her head like glue. The bottom of the cotton was now bound to the head like hair but whoever it was kept rubbing, making it feel like Peebles had hair that someone was yanking on.

"Clemat?" Pebbles asked as she popped her head out of the ground like a mole.

Clemat sat next to the hole Pebbles was in. He was holding the top of the cotton. In front of them, he made a few more cloud lights and planted them close together in the ground. Making a campfire with no heat.

"You, okay?" He asked, concerned.

"Yeah…" Pebbles replied while she struggled to get out of her hole. "Better now."

Clemat extended his hand to help Pebbles up.

"It's too dark to keep going, so let's just set up camp here." He said as he pulled her up. He observed the glimmer in Pebbles' hands as it caught the light from the campfire. He shook the image of the rock shards he found and continued, "Have an early start tomorrow."

"Yeah ... Okay..."

The moment Pebbles got up, she hugged Clemat tight, squeezing him with those smooth rock arms. He squeezed back, feeling his shirt growing damp

****

They both sat around camp, Clemat twisted a cotton bundle to take the few sips of water is released. He then reached into his jacket to take out another energy bar.

"Five more, hope I get to a place with food I can eat next time."

"What do you mean? Oh yeah, how did you...?"

"I don't know," Clemat said as he ripped open the packet and took a bite. "I just... blipped."

"Blipped? You have no control of where you go?"

"Or when."

"And that doesn't concern you?!" Pebbles raised her voice a little. The thought of being in Clemat's position made her queasy.

"Well of course it does, but there's not much I can do about it." He shrugged. "Just need to keep moving forward and hope I find the answer."

They both fell silent. Clemat wished he knew more, knew why this was happening. Though there was a part of him that was afraid of finding out. He liked the adventure, it scares him, but he likes it.

He could see the wheels in Pebbles' head turned through her expressions.

"How do you do that?" Pebbles finally asked.

"What? This?" Clemat pointed to his chewing. "Well, I..."

"No, how do you just keep moving forward? I don't get it..." Pebbles cut him off, her voice grew desperate. "I froze back there, LITERALLY dug a hole for myself... I thought I was an adventurer... that I was brave..."

Another pause while Clemat swallows what was thrown at him. And also, the energy bar.

"Maybe that's why the town doesn't have confidence in me..." Pebbles finished.

Clemat paused. He remembered Rockford's words. The impact that has on the entire narrative.

"Well, I... I just move." Clemat said slowly, he tried his best to find the right words. "If I just keep moving, I'll get somewhere. So instead of waiting around for an answer, I'll know if I'm right or wrong sooner..."

Clemat looked at Pebbles, putting his hand on her shoulder.

"And you are an adventurer, you've already made it this far." He continued. "Quite literally, barely anyone else in your town has attempted what you're doing. You just need a little more experience."

Pebbles smiled and thanked him. She plucked at the grass while staring at the fire. As she plucked on, she weaved them together.

"Do you at least know how it started?" Pebbles pressed further. "Was it your choice?"

"I can't remember," Clemat said, looking directly into the cluster of lights that made up their campfire. "Everything seems unnaturally hazy. Like, I barely remember the first couple of worlds I've been blipped to, but my memory seems to be sticking as time goes on."

"What if you blip away tonight and I'm left alone?"

That caught Clemat off guard. He didn't expect to blip this early. From experience, it normally took a couple of days.

"Then you continue on your journey. I'll be sorry I can't go with you, but I'll also be super hungry and hoping there's food at the other place." He chuckled.

Pebbles crawled over and sat next to Clemat. She took his left hand and slid a grass cuff that she was weaving onto his wrist. The cuff was linked with a grass chain that ended with another cuff on her wrist.

"Smart one P!" Clemat said as he understood what Pebbles was trying to do. He observed the cuff on his wrist, admiring the craftsmanship behind it.

"This way, I might be able to hold you back from leaving unintentionally."

"I would love that! Besides, even if this doesn't work…"

"It'll work." Pebbles said, oddly confident.

"I think you are smart enough to be an adventurer," Clemat said with a smile.

<u>Chapter Eleven</u>

When the sky regained its glow, the two of them continued walking and planting the cloud lights in the ground. However, they are going way slower than usual. At their speed, the swirls of the cotton trees seemed almost gentle that it could be mistaken for the wind.

Clemat was at the front holding on to the bag, stuffing the lights into the cotton and passing it back to Pebbles. She then dug the holes and planted the lights.

The grass chain bound them together. So, it could never let them be more than a few feet away from each other.

She was pretty relieved that Clemat was still here, believing that the grass chain worked in making that happen.

"Gosh, this is taking FOREVER!" Clemat said loudly.

"Quiet down…" Pebbles shushed. "The Gramoglogen might hear us."

Clemat looked at the cuff on his wrist. It made them both feel comfortable knowing that they won't be separated by the demon of the forest again. Though it didn't help that they were moving at a snail's pace.

"That won't happen, it just responds to our movements, I think…" Clemat said, irritated. "Why… why can't it respond to LITERALLY ANYTHING ELSE!? Wish I could see what's making the trees swirl instead of just the trees."

"Cliff said that if the Gramoglogen sees us, it'll come charging at us."

"Mmm… yea, but still, we won't make the deadline otherwise."

Pebbles still felt uneasy with the danger but didn't argue, it would be counterproductive to make more noise than necessary.

Intentionally, Clemat avoided the trees that he hid behind. Since he was leading the way, he made sure those stone shards were out of sight. He couldn't risk Pebbles seeing them. He couldn't risk seeing them again.

As they gradually moved forward, the swirling maintained its slow speed. Though the more time passes, the closer to them it feels.

To keep his mind off things, Clemat continued making jokes and stuffing the cloud lights until the bag was stocked up with them. While in the background, Pebbles grabbed them from Clemat's back and planted them in the ground, giggling and making jokes of her own.

"Y'know what would be cool?" Clemat asked. "A room where anything you asked for just appears right in front of you without delay. That would be awesome."

"What? Why? Then you'll never leave the room."

"That's the point!"

"What if you wanted fresh air? Will the room just fart in your face…" Pebbles fell silent and stopped walking. Clemat was yanked back by the chain.

"P? What happened?" Clemat quickly turned back to face Pebbles. She had a dead stare just slightly off to the front of them. He then tracked Pebbles' gaze. Eventually locking eyes with the fabled demon of the forest.

The creature was as big as Rockford was. It had four thick black hooves. The body had the appearance of the surrounding trees and it had three horns that looked like tougher and sharper branches sticking out of its head. Aside from the horns, it looked like…

"A FREAKING GOAT?!" Clemat shouted, bewildered, and confused.

The goat charged at them, Clemat tried to run but Pebbles decided to root herself to the ground again, causing a ring of light to appear beneath her.

"P! We NEED to go!" Clemat was shouting in a panic. "The thing is running towards us!"

Pebbles didn't budge.

"No, we just need to stay still, the Gramoglogen will leave us alone if we don't move!"

"It saw us! That's not how it works!"

Without missing a beat, more goats appeared and started charging towards them, a whole herd. From Clemat and Pebbles' point of view, it looked like the forest was converging on them.

Clemat was getting desperate, he hopped onto Pebbles' head, trying to keep his balance.

At that moment, the first goat rammed its head into the front of Pebbles, then one from the side and behind until they were surrounded by a sea of goats.

The bleats and pattering hooves from the goats were so loud that Clemat's ears rang. The noise at such proximity was giving him a splitting headache. The back of his neck also started feeling warm.

"Are you ok?" Clemat shouted. "Sorry, I can't exactly root myself to the ground."

"I'm... I'm... fine." Pebbles said though she was clearly struggling. "We just need to bear with this for a bit, they will see that we aren't moving and leave."

The ramming continued, the sound of hooves on the ground dominating the area with the occasional howl and bleats from the goats. Their wolf-like howls made their cotton coats and surrounding trees shiver, making the sea of cotton look like it's going through a hurricane.

Clemat looked around, trying to find a way out. He noticed that Pebbles was starting to crack from the continuous ramming. With every hit, the cracks got deeper and wider, revealing the little glimmers inside as the light refracted on it.

"This isn't working! I'm going to do something, get ready!"

"Clem?" Pebbles said as she winced from the pain.

Clemat took the bag off his back, opened the flap and flailed it around. All the cloud lights on the inside flew out into the sky and floated down and away from them.

The goats slowed their ramming, confused by the sudden movement of everything around them.

When the bag was empty and a little patch cleared, Clemat hopped off Pebbles.

"PEBBLES! We need to go!" He pulled her arm as hard as he could. "NOW!"

Pebbles uprooted herself and they ran as fast as they could. Pebbles looked back; some goats were chasing them while others were distracted by the floating cloud lights.

"Almost there!" Clemat shouted as he struggled to catch his breath.

The clearing on the other side of the forest was making itself visible. Pebbles looked back once again to see that there were three goats still after them and the gap was closing.

A few paces before exiting the forest, Clemat made a quick one-eighty and threw the empty bag at them. It momentarily distracted and slowed them down.

Once Clemat and Pebbles got out of the forest, they hid behind a tree on the last row and stood completely still.

The goats came close, walked around but never exited the forest. It felt like hours but eventually, the goats returned deep into the forest once again.

Both of them sank to the ground and sighed with relief. Once they gathered themselves, they looked up. Finding themselves at the foot of a large, imposing and smooth mountain.

Chapter Twelve

The both of them stood at the edge of the forest, bound together by the grass-weaved chain. A little over ten feet in front of them was a mountain large enough to be both intimidating and awe-inspiring.

The problem hit both of them immediately, the mountain's face was smooth, shining almost. It was the colour of obsidian with the reflective properties of fogged up glass. Closer inspection revealed that it was likely made out of the same materials as Pebbles and the rock people.

Clemat, as he usually did, walked forward, trying to conduct a closer examination. He reached his palm out, wanting to place it on the mountain. Not even four steps forward and his left wrist tugged back.

Pebbles, as she usually did, stood still.

"What's happening? Are those goats after us again?" He quickly turned back, panic rushing to his head again.

Pebbles looked down at the ground. She was reeling from the experience. Her fists were clenched tight, and her feet stuck firmly to the ground.

"Hey..." Clemat said, trying to break the silence.

"Why would you do that?!" Pebbles snapped.

"Do what?"

"Why would you throw away EVERYTHING we have!" Her voice grew louder and more aggressive.

"Oh, you mean save our lives?" Clemat snapped back, not amused with the tone shift.

"We could have handled it! Waited until they tried themselves out or came up with a better..."

"Better what? A better plan?" Clemat interrupted. "There was NO better plan! You were cracking! You could have shatter..."

"There will always be a better plan! But you just keep rushing towards anything that moves! Just like those beasts!"

Pebbles was furious. She walked forward towards the mountain, yanking Clemat along.

"We were in danger! I had to do something! You may be able to take a couple of hits from those guys, BUT NOT FOR LONG! Also, I'm NOT MADE OF STONE!"

Clemat overtook Pebbles and walked in front of her. They were both now up against the mountain. Its smoothness refracted off the green grass, purple sky and orange clouds, giving it a conflicting shimmer.

"You were on top of me! You would have been fine! Now, look!" She gestured at the mountain, her finger almost reflecting off it. "We are LITERALLY at rock bottom with no way of ever climbing up there!"

"But you were cracking!" Clemat said, eyes locked on the cracked lines across her head and arms.

"There's no way of climbing up there, we can't go back, the village is going to come towards us, and they will be destroyed by the Gramoglogen!" Pebbles shouted as she smacked her hand on the face of the mountain.

"Stop dwelling on the past! We got out of there and we will get up there! This is ONLY the second day! You can't be an adventurer if you REFUSE TO MOVE!"

There was a beat... a silence.

Pebbles sat down, back against the mountain, casting a dark shadow on the spot behind her.

Clemat froze from the impact of his words, he hurt Pebbles' already low confidence and dashed her dreams literally against a large rock. But he said nothing more. He was still angry. He saved their lives! He had nothing to apologise for.

He looked away, back towards the forest.

"I know you are against the clock, more so than I am..." Pebbles broke the silence, stared up at the darkening sky above them.

She stopped.

Clemat looked back at her. He thought she was going to apologise.

"But right now," She continued. "I need you to meet me where I'm at. It's a selfish request, I know that. Because... if you keep moving forward and just blip... if this thing..."

Pebbles held up her hand with the grass cuff.

"If this doesn't hold us together... then... I'll have lost... everything..."

Clemat realised what he had done. Pebbles was thinking beyond what was in front of them. After he blips, his actions would have left Pebbles alone, with no resources. She had to face the consequences of his actions.

He sat down next to her. And as golden hour approaches once again, they both just took the time to soak it all in, at rock bottom.

Chapter Thirteen

Some time passed and they both sat at the base of the mountain. The darkening sky cast a purplish shine on the mountain face causing its sparkle to change in hue.

The wind blew gently, rustling Clemat's hair and the grass around him. The cotton on the cotton trees in front of them swayed out of sync with the rest of its surroundings.

Clemat struggled to keep his paper down as he wrote, scribbled, and crudely drew in his little journal.

The winds frustrated him enough to pique Pebbles' interest.

She looked over his shoulder to see that he had been gathering information about the land. Bad drawings of the Gramoglogen, the coconut houses and notes around those drawings.

Clemat noticed Pebbles staring and turned to face her, opening up his book to a page with the Forever Stalk on it.

"You are right, y'know," Clemat said as he struggled to keep eye contact with Pebbles. "This is the fourth world I've been to and yet this is the only one I know the most about."

"Even more than the world of dead grass?"

"Yea, more than the world of hay." He chuckled. "I can't even blame it on the blipping, I just tend to act this way naturally..."

He scribbled more in his notebook.

"Still don't think it's a bad trait though, I just never want to be stagnant." Clemat continued. "But you're right, I need to slow down sometimes. In my attempt to see everything, I saw nothing... Like this mountain here, it's basically you but shiner."

Pebbles smiled. She knew he wasn't just talking about the environment; she knew that he understood how much she needed him to show empathy and patience. She admired him as he continued the last of his scribbles. Even when they are still, he couldn't stop moving.

"Alright, I got a plan." Pebbles said as she stood up and dusted herself off.

"Great! Cause I couldn't think of any."

They walked back towards the forest and peeked inside, confirming that it was calm. They slowly headed in again, pausing every time the trees rustled. They stayed close together as well, walking side by side while keeping an eye on each other's backs.

By the time night fell, they reached the spot where Clemat threw the bag.

Pebbles picked it up, and as expected, it was totally empty inside. They hobbled back to the exit and Pebbles got onto Clemat's back this time. Her cracks were getting larger, and she winced with every step.

"Are you going to be alright?"

"Yeah, let's get through this." Pebbles said.

When they got out of the forest again, they remained in that position, Pebbles on top of Clemat. This reached them high enough to harvest enough cotton to fill up the bag.

When they were done, Pebbles got off and Clemat stretched. She was so much heavier than he expected, and he was expecting a boulder on his shoulders. They both then headed back to the foot of the mountain to take a seat again.

Pebbles taught Clemat how to weave grass and they made short ropes to lace the cotton to their hands and the soles of their feet.

"You ready?" Pebbles asked.

A beat and a deep breath later.

"No, let's rest," Clemat responded with a smile. "It's been a long day."

****

The next morning, Clemat woke up before Pebbles. He observed the glow under Pebbles, as she slept, crept up and softly illuminated her cracks from the inside. He also noticed that they are shallower than what it was the night before.

When Pebbles woke up, Clemat finished up another couple of energy bars and asked, "Are you ready?"

"Yea." Pebbles said with a smile.

After reequipping their makeshift cotton soles and hand pads from the night before, took a deep stable breath, knowing that it might be the last they can have for a while. They both, still bound together by their grass chain, then started rubbing the cotton on the mountain.

Like Pebbles expected, static started to form and eventually the cotton stuck hard to the mountain. She tugged on the bag, now full of cotton again on her back, with glee.

"It works!"

"Let's hope it works all the way up there," Clemat said, nervous at the thought of vertically scaling a mountain.

They both looked up at what awaited them and began their climb. Static cotton suction cups bound to their limbs.

Chapter Fourteen

The both of them have been climbing for a couple of hours, gradually passing midday. Putting one hand in front of the other, they made sure to rub the mountain before trusting it with their weight.

They also had to move at a rather quick speed as the static, generated between the cotton and the mountain face, lost its charge fairly quickly.

Pebbles seemed to be doing fine, her cracks didn't hurt as much as they used to, and the goal was just insight. Clemat on the other hand, literally on Pebbles' right hand, struggled and trailed slightly behind.

"Hey P?"

"Yea...?" Pebbles responded with a quiver in her voice, though not as obvious as Clemat's.

"I don't think my diet of energy bars is helping me out here…"

"Are you okay?" She tried to look back at him but as she did, a huge gust of wind blew past, forcing her eyes shut while she braced herself.

"No…" Clemat said while he braced himself as well. "How much longer till we get there?"

He struggled to hold himself up so much that he couldn't look beyond his next reach. Though he kept moving, slowly but surely catching up to Pebbles, letting the forward momentum carry him.

"Still a little way off, we are barely halfway there."

"Oh, man."

"Are you okay?" Pebbles asked again. "Do you want to stop?"

"What? We can't stop, we'll fall." Clemat responded, his voice as shaky as his limbs. "I don't know how your rock body works, but I'll die…"

They continued, their pace getting slower as the clouds blew in through the sea breeze behind them.

Eventually, Pebbles could feel the tension on the grass chain. Clemat stopped moving and was tugging on it lightly.

"P... I can't... my limbs won't pull me up anymore."

He was stuck there, arms and legs trembling, but not just from the pain and fatigue. The fear of falling got stronger, he was feeling dizzy from exhaustion and dehydration. Once again, the back of his neck started to heat up, a particular spot burning hotter than the rest.

"We... we can..." Pebbles struggled to find a solution. The gears in her head were also slowed from exhaustion.

"...P ..."

Before Pebbles could think of something, Clemat slipped, his right leg lost static from staying still for too long. He slid down the face of the mountain, the shiny and glittering surface streaked like strobe lights right before his eyes.

Clemat tried his best to lean his weight on the mountain. He hoped the friction would help regain some charge, but to no avail. The little amount of charge it gained lost itself so quickly that the drag and jerking motion from his leg caused the other cotton suctions to lose charge as well.

He fell, his back felt like it was pushing away the air cushion behind him. The pieces of cotton strapped to his legs became undone and floated gently to the ground.

But before he fell long, his arm felt a strong tug.

"Ow!" He cried out.

"Ugh!" Pebbles reacted the same.

The grass chain. The link that bound them. The weave was strong enough to now hold them together.

Pebbles' grip on her cotton pads were fading but the charge kept them from detaching from the mountain. And she had the added benefit of having static between her hand and the cotton as well.

"I'm dead oh gosh I'm dead...." Clemat freaked out. "I'm.... de...live? HA! I'M ALIVE! BEAT THAT GRAVITY!'"

"Hey!" Pebbles shouted back at him. "Stop swinging around so much! We don't know how long the chain will hold! We need to think of something now... like before my cotton stops sticking?"

He tired to slow himself down by leaning against the mountain. Allowing the friction to stop his swinging. Pebbles gave a little sigh of relief as she continued to move up a little at a time to keep from losing charge in her cotton pieces as well.

Clemat then shifted his weight back toward the mountain and rubbed the cotton on both his arms to keep himself steady. When those stuck hard, he tried to put his cotton-less shoes on the wall, but they slipped down immediately...

"Okay, that... didn't work... Do you want to pass me another cotton ball for my feet?"

"How am I supposed to do that? My hands are kind of busy... Also, there's no way for you to attach it..."

Pebbles have to keep moving or lose charge and fall too.

Every time she did, she pulled Clemat up as well while he used the momentum to quickly rub his next arm on the wall to stick. His now dangling legs gave a little push before they slipped again. This caused them to constantly brace themselves from the weight of his slips.

"This... isn't working." Clemat chimed in. "It's taking more energy out from the both of us..."

"Both... of us..."

"Yea, that's what I just said."

Pebbles climbed down, back towards Clemat.

"You are going the wrong way," Clemat said, confused with Pebbles' actions.

"I got an idea, Clem, stay still."

He listened. He trusted her confidence as the cotton pads on his hands slowly peel back from the lack of charge again. She got below him and backed up till her head was between his feet.

"Okay, just like in the forest, rest your feet on me." Pebbles explained. "I'll be the legs and support for the both of us, you just focus your energy on pulling us up."

"You sure about that?" Clemat said, feeling guilty. "Seems like an unfair burden on you."

"I know this will work, if you put your legs between the bag straps, you will be pulling me up as much as I'm pushing."

Clemat put his sneakers on Pebbles' shoulders and through the bag strap while Pebbles got into position, making them feel like a unit.

"Ok, this looks super dumb," Clemat remarked. "But... let's... let's make this work!"

Chapter Fifteen

The clouds darkened, paired up with the deep purplish sky. Golden hour was upon them once again. The little glistening of the mountain face guided them as its hue changed in reflection to its surroundings.

The mountain gave off a light sparkle of green, blue and purple at certain angles. As if someone fossilized a tub of glitter and carved it into the shape of a mountain.

Clemat and Pebbles were both shaking, clearly scaling a mountain this way was not fully thought through. The both of them fell silent a long while ago. Partly to conserve energy, partly to not burden the other.

"Please let me stay," Clemat muttered to himself in an attempt to keep his mind off his numbed limbs. "I'll find food somehow. Just let me stay."

The air got colder the higher up they reached. His arms continued to shake violently, but he felt no pain anymore, just repetitive motion carried by momentum.

Over this mountain, over this mountain and there will be food.... the coconuts that they turned into houses must come from somewhere... just a little more... over this mountain.

Clemat started thinking of theories, of why he blipped, how it happened and if it was somehow his choice. Four worlds, one civilisation, none with liveable amounts of food and water.

Pebbles, just below him, supported their weight. With every step, she pushed them up while Clemat pulled. That was the crux of the plan, they supported each other till a point where they can each focus on their task.

It was comforting.

****

It was scary.

"What happens when Clemat blips? This won't last forever." Pebbles muttered as well. "Would I be able to survive on my own? Or would I bury myself alive again?"

These questions swirled around her mind as her shoulders trembled. Her cracks widened a little with the stress they've endured on this vertical scale. Though Pebbles didn't notice as the fear of falling overtook any other sensation.

She wondered if she would have turned out differently if her parents trusted her more? *They trusted Clem to make this trip with me even though they just met him. They made the right choice.... but where does that leave me?*

Pebbles knew that Clemat's time here was going to end inevitably. She tried to justify her fear, maybe it was the way she was raised or maybe the assurance Clemat brought. She was afraid that she was the problem, that has all the trust and confidence in the world would just reveal that she wasn't cut out for it.

I'll show them, I'll show them that they can trust me, just to get to the top of this mountain to do so... She tried to hype herself back up. *Just got to.*

They both climbed, the wind made it harder for them the higher they got. Forcing them to constantly stop and brace themselves.

From their set up, Pebbles could feel Clemat tremble, though she wasn't sure if it was herself that was shaking. She looked back down to see how far they've climbed.

"P!" Clemat shouted as a large dandelion flew by and slammed onto the mountain.

Followed by another, and another. They were sitting ducks and readied themself for impact.

<u>Chapter Sixteen</u>

The large dandelions came one after another, slamming onto the mountain then floating away again. Over and over and over. The duo was stuck in the middle as the wind made it hard to discern a pattern to the fluffy seeds of doom.

Clemat and Pebbles continued to brace themselves, moving around occasionally to avoid the dandelions and to keep from falling. Though this wasn't enough, and their cotton pads were losing charge.

"Woah," Clemat shouted as the base of the dandelion slammed right next to his head. He felt the impact blows and vibrations on the mountain. As it floated away, he sighed with momentary relief. If the dandelion floated lower, the fluffy end would have knocked both him and Pebbles off.

Though, that relief was short-lived as the bombardment continued.

Clemat looked down at Pebbles who was struggling to keep them up. His movements to avoid impact were causing strains on the cotton suction cups.

Pebbles groaned; her eyes shut tight as if preparing for the worst. She felt the impact of that dandelion that landed next to Clemat too. It reverberated throughout her body.

Slowly, she opened her eyes and looked up. They both locked eyes, giving each other a concerned look.

There was another strong gust of wind that blew from the left of them. They both turned to face it, preparing to move out of the next dandelion's way. But all they saw was a dandelion kissing the mountain, sliding, and making its way towards them.

Clemat started to climb and pull the both of them up. His arms were no longer tired, body pumped full of adrenaline. Pebbles felt the tug on the bag straps and immediately followed suit. They climbed as fast as they could, hoping they could out speed the dandelion windshield wiper heading toward them.

Within seconds, the top of the dandelion with its many bristles, made contact with Pebbles' legs, pushing her off balance and causing her to swing back along the path of the dandelion.

Clemat struggled to hold the both of them up. He dug his legs into the bag straps while using all his energy to pull himself and Pebbles up. He let out a loud grunt as they slipped down ever so slightly.

Pebbles released her left hand from the cotton's static grasp and allowed her body to swing further. She then grabbed onto one of the many florets on the dandelion. Using her swinging momentum, she pulled the dandelion along and changed its path away from sweeping the mountain face.

The dandelion was caught by another gust of wind which took it off its course.

"P! Time to hook back now!" Clemat shouted as beads of his sweat dripped down on and past her.

She swung back and leaned her weight toward the mountain. Using the momentum once again, she pushed the cotton pads on her two feet and left hand on the mountain. Rubbing the two surfaces together furiously as she did which caused it to gain just enough static to solidify her position.

"That was really cool!" Clemat said with a shaky voice.

Pebbles smiled but didn't say anything in return. She was still looking around, only to find more heading their way.

They both looked up, trying to see how far they had left to go. To their dismay, the peak was still not visible. All they saw was the shiny mountain face and the rouge dandelions floating about above them.

Their pieces of cotton started to peel as they caught their breath; they have been idle for too long. They could both feel themselves ever so slightly detaching and sliding downward.

The both of them looked at each other and around them for any help while trying to rub and preserve as much charge as possible.

"Clem!"

"I'm thinking about the same thing!"

They both smiled and gave each other a knowing nod.

And jumped.

They fell, still holding formation. The breeze violently shuffled Clemat's hair and jacket. They kept falling but they both laughed.

Before long, their formation broke, though they still kept close with the grass link. Pebbles held tight to the bag while Clemat kept his eye on the target. Without much adjustment, they landed on the hilt of a dandelion that had a course toward the mountain.

There they were again, on another dandelion with Pebbles further up ahead and Clemat behind. Now, they had practice.

Pebbles pulled the head of the dandelion, so it edged upward, catching the draft to gain more height. Clemat took charge of steering, angling the tail so they headed in a straight line and not face-first into a giant slab of rock.

Soon, they were high enough to see the peak.

"There it is!" Pebbles exclaimed.

"Home stretch!" Clemat chimed in. "Let's bring it in close..."

Before he could finish, another dandelion made contact. In the brief moment that they were distracted, it brushed past, causing their dandelion to spin uncontrollably. They were quickly getting off course with no way of regaining control.

The constant winds that high up were doing them no favours. They could see all their progress spiralling further and further away.

"You ready?" Clemat asked as loud as he could.

"Wait for it!" Pebbles responded.

They both timed it. Right at the moment when they spun facing the mountain, they leapt off the dandelion once again. They both dived toward the mountain, Pebbles angled herself below Clemat so they could go back into their previous formation.

Pebbles struggled to grab onto Clemat's legs while he kept his vision peeled on their target. But before they could fully coordinate that during a free fall, Clemat yanked the bag off Pebbles. He held it close to his chest, strapped it onto himself and aimed toward the mountain.

They slammed right into it, knocking the breaths out of their chest. They recoiled and bounced a couple of times before they made consistent contact with the mountain. As they slid down, the cotton within the grass bag developed enough static to hold them both up.

With Clemat having the bag strapped to his chest and Pebbles holding onto his legs. Pebbles then furiously rubbed her legs on the mountain to develop charge and to gain them more stability.

"Ha HA!" Clemat was ecstatic! "I can't believe that worked! We're ALIVE!"

"That was amazing, Clem!" Pebbles couldn't help but shout out as well. "We are so high up now!"

"Just a little more! Let's keep going, P!"

Golden hour faded as they climbed the final stretch of the mountain. The sky went completely dark and not a single cloud hung over them. The shimmering mountain face continued to guide them up, bit by bit.

Before long, the peak was within reach. Before long, Clemat's hand reached a ledge. Using the last of his energy, he pulled the both of them up.

"We...WE'RE HERE! WE'RE HERE!"

He untangled himself from the backpack straps to prop his body over the ledge. After he safely got up there, Clemat leaned over and extended his hand to pull Pebbles up.

"We did it, P," Clemat said, a mixture of pride and exhaustion in his tone.

"We made it." Pebbles replied. "The top of the world."

Chapter Seventeen

Both of them stared beyond the mountain. Though it was dark, they stood there in awe of the vastness that is the land beyond. Trying to look for the non-existent wall in the distance.

To their right was a lake, so large that it could fit the whole town in. The lake itself gave off a blue and yellow sparkle. They weren't sure if it was the stuff living in the lake or the lake itself, but it illuminated the surrounding area.

At the end of the lake closest to the mountain laid two rivers diverging after a point. Its starting point was unknown as the light from the lake got dimmer the further away it got from the source. Oddly enough, the water from the faraway river didn't carry the same light as the lake, causing it to disappear into the darkness.

To their left, they noticed a huge looming monument. It might be a tower or another mountain. At the top, there were orange lights, clearly, those made from the clouds. Those lights trailed the monument's length, describing its form and showing its intimidating size.

"That's beautiful…" Clemat said, eyes still glued to the scenery beyond him.

"That's it?" Pebbles rebutted.

"What? What do you mean that's it? Are we not looking at the same thing?"

"Yea, we are both looking at nothing. There's only that tiny ocean and another mountain to climb."

"You're excited." Clemat chuckled.

Pebbles paused.

"I am…" She said with a soft smile and joy in her voice. "But I'm also afraid… there's so much to do, so much more to see… do my parents even know about… MY PARENTS!"

Pebbles turned back quickly to see her town beyond the forest. Pebbles could make out their shape by the light totems surrounding them.

"We should signal them."

"No... we can wait until the morning, it's late, Clem, they are probably asleep."

"Just do it," Clemat said with a stern tone. "They are worried."

Pebbles thought for a bit and gave in. She kneeled down to where Clemat placed the grass bag. The front of it was now a little frayed from the friction during the climb. She dug through the bag, careful not to let any stray cotton float off with the wind.

"How... How are we supposed to signal them?" Pebbles said as her rummaging got increasingly intense. "We threw all our lights away in the forest!"

"Oh, yea…" Clemat looked up. "It doesn't look like it's going to rain soon either…"

"Great." Pebbles said in defeat as she closed the bag and plopped it next to her. "We got all the way here just to fail at the last step."

"We haven't failed…" Clemat thought aloud. "Not yet…"

He reached into the bag to grab cotton, squeezed the tiny bits of water out of it and into his mouth. Then reached into his pocket to grab an energy bar.

"Oh wait…"

He pulled out a cloud light from the inner pocket. The one he pocketed on his first night here. After his talk with Rockford.

"You are amazing!" Pebbles jumped.

Pebbles grabbed the light from Clemat and started to signal the town. Using her hands to cover and reveal the light to make a pattern.

Almost immediately, lights started to signal back. First from where it looks like her house was, followed by the rest of the town. One by one, the valley lit up, the soft and beautiful orange glow illuminated the surrounding lands.

"They were waiting! They were waiting for me!" Pebbles hopped.

Tears formed as the signalling went on for a while. Clemat wasn't sure if it was some sort of Morse Code, but he didn't want to break the mood.

He just sat there, happy for Pebbles.

Chapter Eighteen

They set up camp for the night, backs turned against the town. The bag to Pebbles' side and the grass chain binding them in between.

Clemat was lying down, he drifted in and out of sleep. He was exhausted, starving and thirsty. More than he has ever been. At the same time, he was relieved.

Pebbles stared out to the great unknown. She sat with her chin on her knees and drew imaginary circles on the smooth mountain surface below her with her finger. The soft sparkles just beneath its surface reflected off her own.

Following the sparkles, she drew a random pattern, connecting the dots between the same colours. Her finger eventually reached the bag that sat between them. She clasped herself hard with her hands and rested her chin on her knees, feeling a sense of pride and uncertainty.

"Clem?" She checked if he was awake while keeping her gaze locked to the great unknown in front of her.

Clemat shifted to signal that he was awake but didn't make a peep.

"What if I don't want to keep going? What if I want to go back?"

"Then you go back." He replied, eyes still shut.

"But... it's my dream to adventure, it feels dirty that I'm even thinking about this..."

"Look, if you go back." Clemat sat up to meet her distant gaze. "You aren't betraying any dream. It was your choice to go back just like it was your choice to climb up here. Just take charge of it."

Pebbles was deep in thought, trying to process Clemat's words. The contradictory nature of it made it hard to comprehend. She understood the intention, but it still didn't feel right.

"Besides, you know how to get up here now." He continued. "You can always pick up where you left off."

"It's not that easy, Clem." She paused before finishing her train of thought. "If I go back, my parents, the whole town won't trust me anymore. Even less than they normally do. I don't need the whole town... just my parents... if they just trusted me more..."

"Y'know that's not how it works right?"

"Trust? They trusted you the first time they met you! And I did too! We were right to... so why can't they have the same confidence in me?"

"You need to stop beating yourself up." Clemat sighed. "We made it this far because you figured out ways to get us out of trouble again and again. You can't ask someone to trust you, you've gotta trust yourself first."

There was a beat. They both sat there quietly, letting the now gentle breeze calm them.

"Have more confidence in yourself and that'll give them permission to do the same."

Clemat put his hand, the one bound by the grass chain over Pebbles' shoulder. He gave her a tight squeeze. Pebbles didn't resist. She leaned her head into his shoulders.

"It worked on me, P. I saw you solve problems, the joy it brings. Made me trust you way more."

Clemat pulled back and laid back down.

"Thanks, Clem. That helped." Pebbles' soft smile returned.

"Whether you choose to move forward or go back, I'm sure you will do amazing."

Clemat laid back down and let the quiet night overtake his senses. He drifted off to sleep, exhausted from everything that happened.

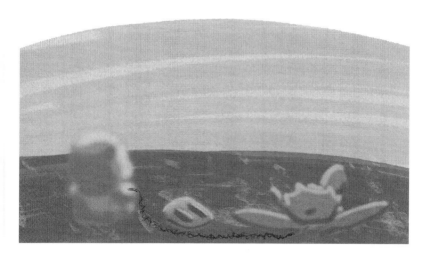

Chapter Nineteen

There was heat on Clemat's face. A heat he hasn't felt since he arrived in the world of rocks and cotton. He opened his eyes slowly as they struggled to gain focus.

A blue sky came into vision with a huge brown rock arch over him.

His exhaustion from before was totally gone, it felt like he was in a deep slumber for at least a couple of days. His hunger and thirst were still there though not as intense as before, which didn't feel natural.

"... Dang"

He sat up slowly and rubbed his head to find that the grass chain was broken. The cuff stayed strong on his wrist, but it was as if the middle link of the weave had been singed apart with fire.

Clemat sat up slowly and looked around him. His surrounding foreign, reddish brown sandstones lined his view with more dunes further off in the distance. Just over the horizon, he noticed a castle, it was too far of a distance to make out the general shapes but large enough to make its presence known.

Though the heat felt dry, the shadow from the arch provided enough shade to even things out. There wasn't a cloud in sight, or any living creatures for that matter.

He wrapped the loose and charred end of the chain around the cuff and his wrist and reached into his pocket for his notebook. He flipped past the pages of notes he took at the base of the mountain and reached his world overview page.

Four crudely drawn earths with numberings #1, #2 and #3. The first three were crossed out. He took out his pen and below the fourth earth, he noted.

PEBBLES' WORLD

Before putting a tiny checkmark beside it.

Clemat stood up slowly, pocketing the notebook and pen once again. He then took off his jacket to brush the sand off his face and hair before tying it around his waist.

Clemat paused.

He looked at the grass cuff and then at his surroundings. He rubbed his neck, feeling a small non-existent burn mark on it which faded gradually.

"Good luck P."

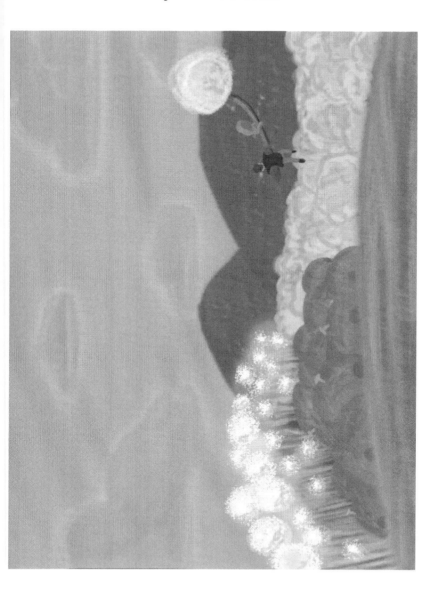

Author's Note

This feels weird. Writing a note for my first book. I've lived with these characters for over a year, writing and re-writing them for different mediums. Though the intended medium might have changed, the story more or less stayed the same.

Converting it from a screenplay to a comic script and now to a short novel. This was just an attempt to fulfil a childhood dream of mine, to have a story out in the world. I only started telling people I was doing this halfway through and it was met with way more support than I anticipated.

Thank you to those who encouraged me. And to those who are new to my work, I really hope you enjoy yourself and have a good time. (or I'll drown myself in ice cream)

Shawn :)

Blip: Rocks and Cotton

Feedback and Links

Twitter: twitter.com/shawn_something
YouTube: youtube.com/shawnsomething
Email: shawnwrotesomething@gmail.com

Blip: Rocks and Cotton

Ok, bye.

Printed in Great Britain
by Amazon

75145522R00073